For Rob, Terry, Marg, Spike the porcupine,
and a giant Sitka spruce near Glacier Bay
K.P.

For all those committed to saving our vanishing rainforests
and for Gary Stolz and my staff: Chris, Colin, Craig, Deirdre,
Erin, Gavriel, Gilbert, Lisa, Mel, and Ray
A.W.

For Eric, who shares his great delight in Nature
with our children, Melina and Jendy
D.Y.T.

Text copyright © 1999 by Karen Pandell • Photo of Robert Davidson on page 4 courtesy of Ulli Steltzer, from *Eagle Transforming* (Vancouver, B.C.: Douglas & McIntyre, 1994). Photo of banana slug on page 22 copyright © Ray Pfortner. Photo of red-backed vole on page 23 copyright © John R. MacGregor/Peter Arnold Inc. All other photographs copyright © 1999 by Art Wolfe • Illustrations copyright © 1999 by Denise Y. Takahashi

*Library of Congress Cataloging-in-Publication Data*

Pandell, Karen.
Journey through the northern rainforest/Karen Pandell; photographs by Art Wolfe;
illustrations by Denise Y. Takahashi. —1st ed.   p. cm.
Summary: Through the eyes of an eagle, the reader explores the ancient, but disappearing, rainforest of the Pacific Northwest.
ISBN 0-525-45804-2 (hc)
1.Rainforests—Pacific, Northwest—Juvenile literature. 2. Rainforest ecology—Pacific, Northwest—Juvenile literature.
[1. Rainforests. 2. Rainforest ecology. 3. Ecology. 4. Eagles.] I. Wolfe, Art, ill. II. Takahashi, Denise Y., ill. III. Title.
QH86.P355 1999 578.734'09795—dc21 99-31646 CIP AC

Published in the United States by Dutton Children's Books,
a division of Penguin Putnam Books for Young Readers
345 Hudson Street, New York, New York 10014
http://www.penguinputnam.com/yreaders/index.htm

Designed by Amy Berniker • Map and diagram by Richard Amari
Printed in Hong Kong   First Edition
1 3 5 7 9 10 8 6 4 2

OVERLEAF: *Bald eagle swooping for prey*

# COASTAL TEMPERATE RAINFORESTS
## OF NORTH AMERICA

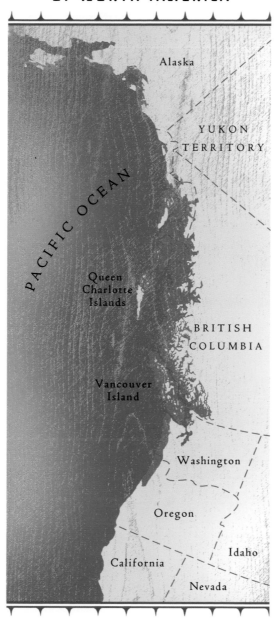

Alaska

YUKON
TERRITORY

PACIFIC OCEAN

Queen
Charlotte
Islands

BRITISH
COLUMBIA

Vancouver
Island

Washington

Oregon

Idaho

California

Nevada

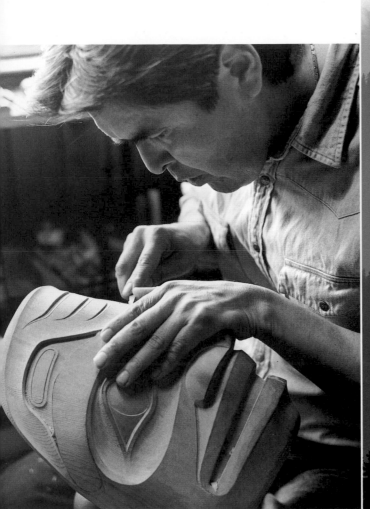

**ROBERT DAVIDSON** is a modern-day Haida (HY-dah) artist. The Haida are one of many Northwest Coast Indian tribes living in the northern rainforest. Davidson carves masks from western red cedar and other rainforest trees. He believes that we are connected to the spirit world through our minds. To create an Eagle, Raven, Bear, or other mask, he must be in touch with the spirit of that creature. Then, after the mask is finished, anybody who wears it will be able to feel the animal's spirit, too.

For many generations, the people native to the ancient forests of the Pacific Northwest have felt a kinship with the animals. Their beliefs have helped them live in harmony with the natural cycles of the trees, salmon, bears, eagles, and other living things in the northern rainforest.

LEFT: *Robert Davidson carving a shark mask*
MIDDLE: *Olympic National Park, Washington*
RIGHT: *Bald eagle*

As a result, this forest has provided them with a never-ending supply of food, water, fuel, and building and craft materials. It also has given them inspiration for dance, music, art, myth, and rituals.

But in today's fast-paced world, these temperate rainforests are rapidly vanishing. Why is this happening, and what can be done to preserve and protect these very special places?

To explore these questions, we'll take an eagle's-eye view of this unique habitat.

**P**ut on an Eagle spirit mask and take a journey into the disappearing world of the northern rainforest. To see through the Eagle's eyes, follow the wooden panels throughout the book.

As a bald eagle, you fly high above the tallest, cathedral-like spires of the evergreen trees. Your black wings span more than six feet. With your keen yellow eyes, you look down at the forest.

The canopy, or top layer, of a temperate rainforest is very different from a tropical-rainforest canopy. In the Tropics, a canopy of dense vegetation usually closes out the sunlight. But the canopy of a northern

*Old-growth rainforest*

rainforest is open. The giant trees narrow at the top, allowing rays of sun to filter all the way down to the forest floor.

**P**ull in your wings and stretch out your yellow talons. You land on the top of a Sitka spruce more than two hundred feet high.

The spiky tops of such tall trees are the first link in the unique water-management system of a northern rainforest. Farther down the trunk, branches fan out like a partially opened umbrella. When rain or fog hits the forest canopy, gravity forces the water down and out onto the lower tree branches.

Each of the hundreds of branches on a giant rainforest tree has thousands of needles. This means that just one ancient tree in the forest is a huge "water catcher." It catches the water droplets in rain and fog with its more than six million needles.

The northern rainforest also could be called a "fog forest." Scientists have discovered that fog is very important to the life of this temperate forest. One fog brings as much water as a drenching rainstorm. Mist collects on the needles, limbs, and trunk of each tree, then drips to the forest floor. This is called "fog drip."

OPPOSITE: *Old-growth rainforest*
ABOVE: *Mist rising over the forest*

With your excellent eagle vision, you catch sight of a marbled murrelet landing on a nest in the hanging garden of a nearby tree.

The hanging gardens of the temperate rainforest soak up water like a sponge. This community of plants develops only after the tree is more than one hundred fifty years old. Such an ancient tree has very wide branches. Mosses, lichen, and ferns can now grow on the branches, which are often more than one hundred fifty feet above the forest floor. These aerial plants absorb all their nutrients from the rain and air instead of from the soil or trees upon which they grow. They are called epiphytes (EP-eh-fites), from a Greek word that means "upon a plant." Birds, such as marbled murrelets and rufous hummingbirds, nest in these hanging gardens. Red tree voles live here, too.

OPPOSITE AND ABOVE LEFT:
  *Moss-covered big-leaf maples*
LEFT: *Lichen on tree branch*
ABOVE RIGHT: *Rufous hummingbirds*

Even a torrent of water turns into a gentle, steady rain by the time it reaches the forest floor. By then the water is purified, too. Like giant filters, the trees remove particles of dirt or other substances.

The temperate rainforest has rain or fog throughout the four seasons. Even the summers are cool and wet, with no real droughts. Rainfall for the whole year averages between eight and thirteen feet.

How did all this rain get here? To understand, think of the weather in the Northern Hemisphere as a giant wheel, rotating clockwise and set in motion by the rays of the sun. It turns under the weight of the atmosphere, which changes in pressure from time to time and place to place.

In the Tropics, near the equator, the sun heats the water of the Pacific. As this happens, moisture evaporates into the air above the sea. When gravity pulls the air downward from areas of high pressure to low, winds are created. The winds, along with the rotation of the earth, then move the warmed-up air and water to the west.

When this air and water reach the area of the Pacific near Japan, they begin to flow northeast. Ultimately, part of this warmer water of the Japan Current, as it is called, hits the Pacific Northwest coast along with the moisture-filled air.

There, high mountains cool and trap the air. The temperature of the air now drops, and as the water cools, it condenses into clouds and fog. Rain begins to fall.

The current then heads south. Off the coast of Mexico, it again travels west to the Tropics. The giant weather wheel is now complete. Throughout the year, this wheel keeps turning and rotating, bringing water to the northern rainforest. During the fall, there are sometimes very big storms.

OPPOSITE: *Rainforest waterfall*

**S**itting on top of a tree, you feel the deluge of water pelting your white head feathers.

When really strong winds push against its trunk, even the biggest rainforest tree can be knocked down. Although mammoth in height, these trees have very shallow root systems. Tree roots in this habitat usually reach down only two or three feet into the soil but may spread more than forty feet across to absorb the dripping rain and fog water.

For thousands of autumns, trees like the one below have come down during severe storms. In fact, biologists say that four out of five of all fallen trees on the forest floor in areas that were not logged fell because of wind rather than old age, disease, or fire.

When a tree crashes to the ground, decay begins quickly. Insects arrive to colonize the log almost immediately. In time, moss, fungi, and lichen cover it, too. The wood softens as it decomposes. It now holds two to three times as much water as it did when it was standing. It has become another "water catcher" in the forest.

*Your eagle talons grasp the treetop tightly as the Sitka spruce sways wildly in the wind.*
*CRASH! You watch a tall nearby tree topple to the ground.*

Soon the fallen tree will become a nursery log. Seeds drop on the moss carpet that covers it. A line of seedlings appears, and the seedlings grow into young trees. Over centuries they will form a graceful colonnade of rainforest giants.

In the northern rainforest, living things are constantly recycled. Some of this recycling requires a very long time. Biologists estimate that a northern rainforest tree takes as many centuries to decay as it did to grow.

OPPOSITE: *Fallen tree decaying*
TOP: *Hemlock trees growing on a nursery log*
BOTTOM LEFT: *Mushroom in decaying leaves*
BOTTOM RIGHT: *Lichen on the rainforest floor*

Many creatures such as raccoons, mice, otters, skunks, weasels, and salamanders make a home inside or under the nursery log as it rots. Chipmunks and squirrels may cache food for winter in it. Birds, such as the winter wren, will use the top of the log as a perch. Other animals will use it as either a tunnel to travel through or a bridge to travel across the tangled vegetation on the rainforest floor.

Perched on the tree, you catch sight of an animal's tail as it disappears into the nursery log.

OPPOSITE LEFT: *Bald eagle on nest*
OPPOSITE RIGHT: *Raccoon*
TOP: *Spotted owl catching a mouse*
MIDDLE: *River otters*
LEFT: *Northern red-legged frog*

A salmon spends one to five years in the ocean. Near the end of its life, however, each fish returns to the same freshwater stream in the rainforest where it was hatched. At this time, a female salmon will fan the gravel bed in the water with her tail to make a redd, or nest. Here she lays thousands of eggs. A male salmon fertilizes these eggs. This is called spawning.

*Salmon! Your sharp eagle eyes have spotted many bright red fish swimming up a stream.*

Each year, the fish that are ready to spawn gather in great numbers in a "salmon run." The wild salmon in each rainforest stream have inherited special traits from their ancestors that fit the particular conditions in each stream. For example, some salmon had to swim upstream over waterfalls to reach their spawning area. These salmon became good jumpers. Others had to pass through rapids. These fish became really powerful swimmers. Some had to travel up very long freshwater streams to spawn deep in the rainforest. They developed much endurance.

Such traits are passed on over thousands of years by the salmon that return to each stream. If a stream remains undisturbed and protected, then the survival of hundreds, then thousands, and, over time, millions of fish is ensured.

*Leaving your perch, you fly, talons poised and ready, to catch one of the salmon. Splash! Off you go with the fish wriggling in your clutches.*

Theirs is a truly amazing migration. In some mysterious way, the salmon know how to find their way home to spawn after swimming great distances in the sea. Some of these fish have been known to travel nearly ten thousand miles!

However, biologists have begun to solve one part of this puzzle. They believe that a baby salmon's brain somehow remembers the special smell that makes up the chemical composition of the rocks, vegetation, and water of its own stream. As the young salmon grows, it eventually swims from this stream into a river that leads to the ocean. The smells the fish experiences along the way are registered in certain cells in its brain. This allows the salmon to retrace its journey from the mouth of the river when it is ready to spawn.

OPPOSITE: *Spawning sockeye salmon*
ABOVE: *Close-up of sockeye salmon eggs*

Sometimes when a great tree blows down, it falls across a stream. It then becomes an important part of the life cycle of the wild salmon. The log slows the flow of water in the stream. It creates pools, falls, and eddies for the spawning fish. It also filters out debris, keeping the water clear for the salmon and other fish. And, as it decays, the log slowly releases its stored nutrients into the water.

*As you tear the flesh from the fish with your yellow beak, you watch a bear shinny up a snag, or standing dead tree.*

ABOVE: *Black bear*
RIGHT: *Pileated woodpecker*
OPPOSITE: *Fungus on decaying tree trunk*

Snags are another important aspect of the temperate rainforest. When a tree dies from disease or old age, if not felled by wind or loggers it can remain upright for more than a hundred years. Wood-borers and bark-eating beetles go to work on the snag. Soon they make way for other beetles, ants, and burrowing insects to eat the inner bark layers of the tree. Woodpeckers then come to feed on the insects, drilling larger holes in the trunk. Chestnut-backed chickadees and Vaux's swifts arrive to nest in these holes.

Other creatures find shelter in snags, too. These include spotted owls, flying squirrels, wood ducks, bats, and brown creepers. Fishers, martens, and bobcats seek refuge in the lower levels of the snag. Thus the tree, although dead, supports a great deal of life in the old-growth forest.

In the moss carpet of the forest floor, there is another miniature world. Raindrops are caught and held in this spongy vegetation. Moist and sticky banana slugs leave a trail of mucus as they inch across the ground. They feed on and recycle decaying matter. Slime molds ooze.

A ruffed grouse scurries along the forest floor. The leaves of many flowering plants that bloomed in sequence all spring and summer now turn yellow and red. After the heavier rains and cooler weather of autumn, fungi pop up everywhere.

**A**fter you finish eating the fish, you let its skeleton fall to the ground. It lands quietly on some moss.

Below this layer of mosses and plants, there is even more happening in the rainforest. Some underground fungi called truffles produce small fruiting bodies that look like little potatoes. Truffles grow close to the roots of rainforest trees. This type of fungi receives sugars from the tiny hairlike tips of the roots of the tree. In return, the truffles help the trees take up nutrients from the soil. The fungi release a chemical substance, or enzyme (EN-zime), that enables the tree roots to better absorb the water, minerals, and nitrogen in the soil. This relationship between a tree's roots and the fungi around them is called mycorrhiza (my-ko-RYE-za). Without the aid of these small truffles, there might not be such enormous trees in the northern rainforest!

The truffles have help, too. The red-backed vole scurries around in tunnels and runways in the soil. After it has a tasty meal of truffles, the fungi spores pass through the vole's body undigested. This spreads the spores underground, and new truffles grow from them.

By aiding the truffles, the red-backed vole is also assisting the huge rainforest trees. This is just one example of the amazingly complex web of life in a northern rainforest.

OPPOSITE: *Banana slug*
TOP LEFT: *Fungus on a twig*
TOP RIGHT: *Lichen on the rainforest floor*
BOTTOM: *Red-backed vole*

*SCREECH! You hear a metallic sound in the forest. You cry out in alarm and fly away. Bald eagles, like spotted owls, are disturbed by this noise.*

A bulldozer rumbles into the rainforest. It pushes aside small trees and bushes to make a road.

When the road is finished, loggers come into the forest to cut down the trees.

There are different ways to harvest the trees in a forest. One way is called clear-cutting. In this type of logging, no trees of any age, old or young, are left standing. Even snags are cut down. Since all the giant trees are removed, they will never become nursery logs or a home for wildlife.

As the trees are felled, the nests of birds and animals come down with them.

Hanging gardens, which took more than one hundred fifty years to develop, now lie in shambles on the forest floor.

ABOVE: *Clear-cut of old-growth cedar forest*
OPPOSITE: *Old-growth forest after clear-cutting*

Logged-over land is sometimes burned to remove traces of brush and vegetation. New tree seedlings of a fast-growing type of conifer are then planted by machine in evenly spaced rows. Chemicals are sprayed to kill all "undesirable" wild species of trees, bushes, and flowers that try to grow back.

For the first time in centuries, strong, harsh sunlight directly hits the forest ground. The air temperature rises. The temperature of the water in the stream rises, too.

Young salmon in the first year of their life cannot stand the heat. Many die.

The trees that once acted as natural umbrellas and water catchers to shield the forest from the rains of this climate have vanished. The hanging gardens, which also collected water, are gone.

The rain pelts the forest floor. The moss carpet that once absorbs the water washes away.

Nothing is left to break the force of the water.

Mud slide. You watch a mass of earth shoot down a hill. You are hungry. You fly over to your favorite salmon stream to find a fish to eat. But where are the fish?

As the rain keeps falling, the logging roads become soggy. Pools of muddy water break free and race down a hillside, washing away dirt, rocks, and the pesticides and fertilizers that were sprayed to help the new seedlings grow. The silt, muddy water, and chemicals flow into the stream. The stream begins to flood.

The salmon coming up the stream to spawn have difficulty seeing or even breathing in the water. Most do not spawn. At best, only a few eggs will hatch from this run. If the stream continues to flood and be filled with silt each year, the salmon runs will die out, never to return.

In addition, with no more fish coming back from the sea, other important nutrients for the soil are lost. After the salmon spawn, they die and their bodies decompose, eventually releasing minerals into the soil of the northern rainforest.

With decreasing sources of food and no places to live, many animals and birds must leave their territories.

As they move to new areas of the remaining rainforest, the creatures already living there fight the newcomers. Fewer animal babies are born.

You turn your head back and forth. Everywhere you see animals running and birds flying away.

Even the birds who only visit the rainforest during part of the year are in trouble. The following spring, for example, a hummingbird that flies in from Mexico finds that its favorite nesting site high in the forest canopy is gone. The canopy itself is gone. So there are fewer migrating as well as native birds nesting in the dwindling forest.

With the hanging moss gardens destroyed, the spotted owl has no red tree voles to eat. It is too hungry to nest and raise any young. A marbled murrelet flies in from the sea to lay its eggs. It tries to find a mossy limb on which to nest. But all the mossy limbs are gone.

As the rains continue, more and more nutrients are washed out of the soil. The soil becomes further depleted.

Even the fungi in the soil have long since disappeared. They burned in the brushfires that were set to clear the land.

OPPOSITE: *Logger at work*
ABOVE: *Biologist catching and tagging sockeye salmon*

*You, the Eagle, won't come here again. Your offspring won't either. Soon only a memory is left of the Eagle spirit in what was once the great northern rainforest.*

A diverse natural system, supported by trees of different types, sizes, and ages, once existed here. Decades later, only one species of tree grows in this new tree farm, standing in uniform rows on the hillsides. In this new forest, there isn't a wide variety of places where animals can hide or make homes. Because the trees grow so densely, people no longer come to take nature walks here, either.

*Hiker in old-growth forest*

Over and over again, this scene has been repeated. In just one century, the once continuous and unbroken stretch of old-growth timber has become a series of isolated patches. We have made islands of this ecosystem in the Pacific Northwest. But what does remain includes the largest tracts of some of the rarest rainforest on earth.

*Now take off your Eagle mask and rejoin the world of people interested in what happens to the northern rainforest.*

**Sam Skaggs** and **Richard Carstensen** are freelance naturalists in Juneau, Alaska, who take their own journeys through the northern rainforest. The two tree hunters search for the oldest trees in the Tongass National Forest for their Landmark Tree Project.

It is important work because even the U.S. Department of Agriculture Forest Service, which manages the land, does not know where every ancient tree is located. The tree hunters share their information with the Forest Service and others. Later, they bring people to see the rainforest giants they have discovered.

They know that certain areas they find may be logged. But they believe that more old-growth trees will be saved through their work.

This kind of cooperation will help preserve and protect these forests. Computer modeling, for instance, now makes it possible to coordinate all the human activity that affects them. This means that loggers, fishermen, scientists, environmentalists, miners, Northwest Coast Indians, tourists, and others have the possibility of working together to solve disputes and problems.

We are coming full circle in our thinking at long last. After all, honoring the abundance and biodiversity found in nature has always been central to Northwest Coast Indian beliefs.

We are even rediscovering ancient healing plants found only in this forest. Recently, scientists found that taxol, a substance from the bark of the Pacific yew tree, can successfully treat certain kinds of cancer.

Edward O. Wilson, the eminent Harvard scientist, believes that each of us has biophilia, or an inborn love of living things. We respond to nature because of the DNA in our brains, which evolved from our adaptation to natural surroundings.

Indeed, anyone who lives, works, or walks in the northern rainforest is somehow moved by the presence and power of the ancient trees. In the words of a Tlingit (KLINK-it) elder I once heard in Juneau, "These trees have been here for hundreds of years. Let them live a little longer."

# EXPLORING THE NORTHERN RAINFOREST

The rainforests of the Pacific Northwest draw millions of visitors each year from all over the world. Here are four well-known places where you can walk in the beauty of ancient forests.

**Olympic National Forest** borders Olympic National Park and contains more than 630,000 acres of mountains, streams, and forests on the Olympic Peninsula in Washington. More than 200 miles of trails wind through it. Some connect to Olympic National Park. Two trails loop through the Quinault Rainforest. Please contact: Olympic National Forest Supervisor's Office, 1835 Black Lake Boulevard SW, Suite A, Olympia, WA 98512. (360) 956-2400. www.olympus.net/onf

**Olympic National Park**, also on the Olympic Peninsula, has more than 920,000 acres of wilderness extending from the mountains to the sea. More than 600 miles of trails run through the park. The Hoh Rainforest has several nature trails, including the famed "Hall of Mosses." Please contact: Olympic National Park, 600 East Park Avenue, Port Angeles, WA 98362. (360) 452-0330. www.nps.gov/olym

**Glacier Bay National Park and Preserve** covers more than 3.2 million acres of mountain, glacier, fjord, and forest wilderness. There are no trails other than those around Park Headquarters at Bartlett Cove. These provide a chance to walk in a northern rainforest. Parts of the park border Tongass National Forest. Please contact: Glacier Bay National Park and Preserve, Park Headquarters, P.O. Box 140, Gustavus, AK 99826. (907) 697-2230. www.nps.gov/glba

**Tongass National Forest** is the largest in the United States. It covers nearly 17 million acres in southeast Alaska. However, only about 5 million of these are preserved wilderness, which include Misty Fjords National Monument and Admiralty Island National Monument. In addition to forest ecosystems, many glaciers, ice fields, waterfalls, and fjords are found in Tongass. Man-made trails exist, as well as those made by game. Wilderness cabins may be rented from the Forest Service. Please contact: Forest Service Information Center, 101 Egan Drive, Juneau, AK 99801. (907) 586-8751. www.fs.fed.us/r10/tongass

Other than in North America, these rare temperate rainforests are found only in certain coastal regions of Chile, southern Australia (including Tasmania), and New Zealand. Some ecologists have also identified areas of Norway, Britain, and Japan as temperate rainforests. Let's hope that these areas won't be changing for many years to come.

OPPOSITE: *River in old-growth forest*
OVERLEAF: *Rainbow over Tongass National Forest*

# SAVING THE NORTHERN RAINFOREST

Edward O. Wilson wrote in *The Biophilia Hypothesis* (Island Press, 1993) that "the first 90 percent reduction in area of habitat lowers the species number by one-half. The final 10 percent eliminates the second half."

We are now down to this final and crucial 3 to 10 percent level in the Pacific Northwest of what was once, a hundred years ago, a vast temperate rainforest.

Here are some organizations that help to protect this ecosystem:

## In the United States

Alaska Research Voyages, Inc.
Landmark Tree Project
119 Seward Street, #7
Valentine Building
Juneau, AK 99801
(907) 463-5511
www.alaskavoyages.com

Natural Resources Defense Council
40 West 20th Street
New York, NY 10011
(212)727-2700
www.nrdc.org

Rainforest Action Network
221 Pine Street, Suite 500
San Francisco, CA 94104
(415) 398-4404
www.ran.org

Rainforest Alliance
65 Bleecker Street, 6th floor
New York, NY 10012
(212) 677-1900
www.rainforest-alliance.org

Sierra Club
85 Second Street, 2nd floor
San Francisco, CA 94105
(415) 977-5500
www.sierraclub.org

Save America's Forests
4 Library Court, SE
Washington, DC 20003
(202) 544-9219
www.saveamericasforests.org

## In Canada

Canadian Rainforest Network
207 W. Hastings Street, Suite 703
Vancouver, BC V6B 1H7
(604) 669-4303
www.helix.net/~crn

Sierra Club of British Columbia
P.O. Box 8202
Victoria, BC V8W 3R8
(250) 386-5255
www.sierraclub.ca/bc